Li'l Booger Buddies Inventors Go to School

By Heather Konet

Li'l Booger Buddies Inventors Go to School,
characters, text, images © 2017 Heather Konet, Todd Konet. Li'l Booger character images © 2006, 2009 Heather Konet, Todd Konet.

ISBN-13: 978-1981162512
ISBN-10: 1981162518

For Todd, TJ and Ainsley
Thank you for inspiring me every day.

In a small galaxy far away exists the little green planet of Boogie Woogie, the home of the Li'l Booger Buddies.

The Li'l Booger Buddies are curious creatures who love to make inventions using resources from their planet and junk that they find in outer space.

Most of the space junk is collected by a task team of 4 Li'l Booger Buddies who go on regular missions with the Booger Blaster 4 spaceship.

Other task teams have different responsibilities. One of the most important teams teaches young Li'l Booger Buddies how to invent things at the Boogie Woogie Invent School.

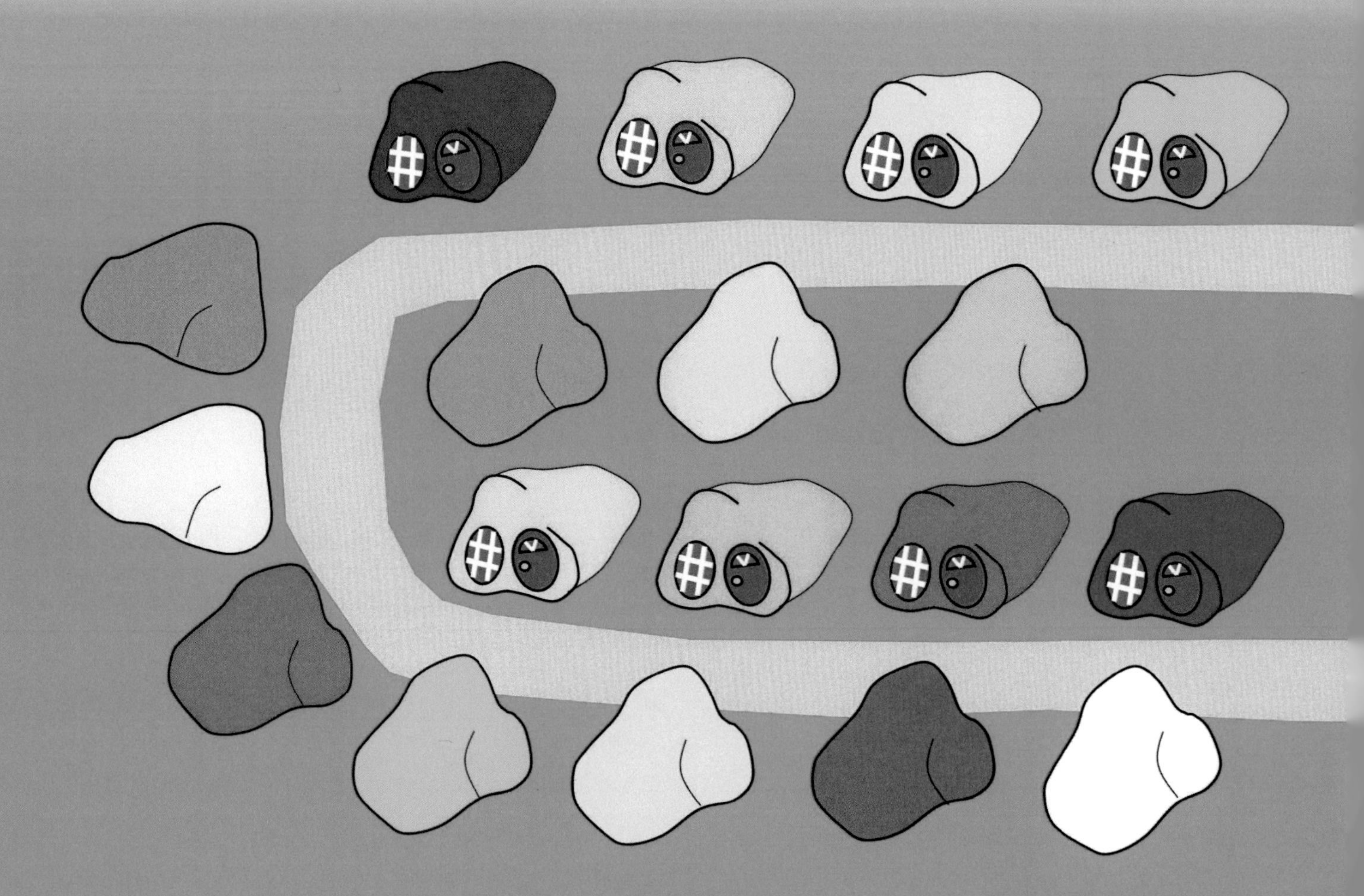

All Li'l Booger Buddies start attending Invent School when they turn 5 years old. The school also welcomes other creatures who are new to the planet.

On Roogie Booger's first day at school she was excited, but also a little scared. After a tour, Roogie and the other new students were brought to their class area. Their teacher, Ms. Soogie, was there to welcome them.

Once the students were seated, Ms. Soogie started the first lesson. She explained that one way to start an invention is to identify a problem that you want to solve. She asked each student to think of a problem and write it down.

Roogie felt nervous and decided that she needed help. She sent a thought to her teacher. Li'l Booger Buddies communicate through their thoughts. Their brains are located in their bellies and glow when they are communicating.

Ms. Soogie told her not to worry. All inventors need help along the way. She gave Roogie a journal to bring home for writing down any problems that she noticed and wanted to solve.

After school, Roogie returned home to her family. Her parents and twin baby sisters were so excited to see her and hear about her first day!

As they sat inside, Roogie explained her assignment and how she couldn't think of a problem to solve. Her Mom kindly suggested that she take a look over at her sisters who were playing on the floor.

Roogie noticed that her baby sisters were fighting over their favorite red ball again. "That's the problem that I should solve!" she thought. She made a note about it in her journal.

The next day at school, Roogie proudly showed her journal to her teacher. Ms. Soogie praised her for identifying a meaningful problem that needed to be solved.

Ms. Soogie explained the next step. She told the students to think of new devices for solving their problem and draw any idea on to paper. Ms. Soogie called this step Brainstorming.

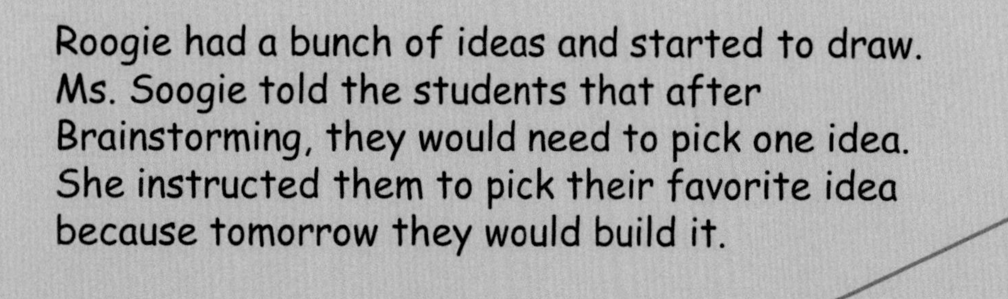

Roogie had a bunch of ideas and started to draw. Ms. Soogie told the students that after Brainstorming, they would need to pick one idea. She instructed them to pick their favorite idea because tomorrow they would build it.

Roogie picked her favorite idea and showed it to her teacher. She couldn't wait to come back to school tomorrow and start building!

When Roogie and the other students arrived at school the next day, Ms. Soogie had materials picked out for them to build their inventions.

Roogie examined the materials and decided on a plan for building. She grabbed some tools and started to build.

After a day of hard work, Roogie completed her invention and showed it to her teacher. Ms. Soogie helped her test it with a ball. The invention worked! Ms. Soogie told her to take it home and determine if it solved the problem.

That evening, Roogie returned home with her invention. She placed her sisters' favorite red ball in it and they happily started playing with it together. She solved the problem!

The next day at school, Roogie told her teacher that her invention was a success. Ms. Soogie congratulated her and gave her a big gold star for completing her first lesson. Roogie thanked her teacher for all of her guidance.

When Roogie returned home that day she was full of pride. She was also happy to see her sisters still playing with her invention! Roogie couldn't wait to get back to Invent School and learn more about inventing.

About the Author:

Heather Konet is a Mom and Automotive Engineer with over 20 patented inventions. She has always loved drawing Li'l Booger Buddies characters and sharing them with family and friends. Heather has combined these passions into stories that aim to make children laugh while introducing them to the fun of inventing.

Made in the USA
Lexington, KY
13 August 2018